The Rescue Princesses
The Enchanted Ruby

Paula Harrison

nosy crow

First published in the UK in 2018 by Nosy Crow Ltd
The Crow's Nest, 14 Baden Place,
Crosby Row, London SE1 1YW

Nosy Crow and associated logos are trademarks and/or registered
trademarks of Nosy Crow Ltd

Text © Paula Harrison, 2018
Cover illustration © Sharon Tancredi, 2018
Interior illustrations © Artful Doodlers, 2018

The right of Paula Harrison to be identified as the author of this work
has been asserted by her in accordance with the Copyright, Designs
and Patents Act, 1988

1 3 5 7 9 10 8 6 4 2

A CIP catalogue record for this book is available from the British Library

Printed and bound in the UK by Clays Ltd, St Ives Plc

Papers used by Nosy Crow are made from wood grown in
sustainable forests.

ISBN: 978 0 85763 908 0

www.nosycrow.com

For Bailey and Taylor,
also known as Squish and Doodles

Chapter One

A Birthday Parcel

Princess Scarlett fizzed with excitement as she ran down the stairs of Bearbrook Castle. She skidded to a halt in the dining room and looked round eagerly. "Has a letter from Ella come today?"

Her mum, Queen Ruth, set down her teacup. "Scarlett, do calm down! Our guests will soon be here to celebrate your birthday tomorrow. What will they think if you're galloping round the castle like a wild pony?"

"Sorry!" Scarlett pushed back the tight black curls that bobbed around her face. "It's just that Ella promised to write another letter. I thought it might come today."

Her mum smiled. "Actually, she's sent you a parcel. It's on the table in the hallway."

"A parcel!" Scarlett's eyes widened. "Can I open it now? I know my birthday isn't till tomorrow but I can't wait to see what's inside."

"All right then." Her mum nodded, smoothing her blue silk dress.

"Thank you!" Scarlett hugged her mum before dashing into the hallway to look for the parcel.

"And slow down a little!" the queen called after her.

Sitting on the hall table was a parcel wrapped in shiny pink paper and tied up with a gold ribbon. The postmark – Harebell Castle – made Scarlett's tummy do a somersault.

Harebell Castle was where Ella, her cousin, went to school – at the Royal Academy for Princesses. Ella had been writing to Scarlett every week describing their picnics and how they looked after the school pets. Scarlett thought it all sounded amazing and couldn't wait until she was old enough to go!

More than anything, she loved Ella's stories about helping animals. Ella had made friends with some other princesses and together they'd made a secret promise to always help animals in trouble. They called themselves the Rescue Princesses, and that name made Scarlett shiver with excitement. They used teamwork and ninja moves to rescue animals, and they even had magic jewels!

Hugging the parcel to her chest, Scarlett ran back up the spiral stairs. Bearbrook Castle was a tall grey palace with an enormous banquet hall and more than fifty bedrooms. Scarlett's room was at the top of one of the towers.

It was crammed with soft toys and had red velvet curtains and a lacy canopy over the bed.

From her window, Scarlett could see the river rushing through the meadow beyond the castle wall. The Kingdom of Deronda was a wild and beautiful land, with snowy mountains, deep forests and sparkling rivers.

Scarlett loved playing in the meadow outside the gate. Sometimes she would see a black bear cub skipping beside its mother on the river bank. If she was very lucky, she would see otters playing in the shallow water. The otters were so adorable, with their sleek furry bodies and bright black eyes!

Sitting down on her bed, Scarlett undid the parcel's gold ribbon and shiny paper. Inside was a card saying *Happy Birthday* with a picture of a birthday cake. There was a letter too and a small wooden box with a gold key.

Scarlett turned the key, lifted the box lid and gasped. A row of silver tools lay neatly

inside. There were several little chisels –
each one a different size – and a tiny silver
hammer. Scarlett's heart skipped a beat. Ella
had mentioned tools like these in her letters.
They were for making the magic jewels that
helped with the animal rescues!

Snatching up the letter, Scarlett read
it eagerly.

Dear Scarlett,

I hope you like your birthday present!!! I know you love
hearing about the Rescue Princesses so I've sent you
some special jewel-making tools. You can use them to make
magic jewels of your own. I asked Jaminta how to make the
jewels magical because she's the best at it. She said first
you should choose the jewel you like most. Then you tap
the hammer against the end of the chisel very carefully and
only chip off a little at a time. The jewels must be shaped
perfectly to release the magic. Jaminta drew a picture on
the back of this letter to show you what she means.

The letter carried on with more news from the Royal Academy for Princesses but Scarlett turned over to study the picture on the back. The drawing showed how to use the tools to make jewels of different shapes.

Scarlett put the paper down and gazed at the tools again. They were so small – just right for shaping precious jewels! Pulling open a drawer, she went through her jewellery. She had two tiaras – a silver one, and a gold one decorated with square emeralds. She also had a diamond flower brooch that her mum had given her, and a sapphire bracelet. None of them seemed quite right though.

She delved below her collection of hair bands until she found a necklace with an oval-shaped ruby at the bottom of the drawer. It was a beautiful gem, as red as a sunset, but it was quite heavy so she hardly ever wore it. It would be perfect for making into a magic jewel!

Carefully, she took the ruby off the gold chain and laid it on her dressing table, before fetching the jewel-making tools. Then she studied the picture on the back of the letter again.

There was a sudden knock at the door and Scarlett looked up in surprise. "Come in!"

Her dad, King Philip, opened the door. He smiled broadly, his dark eyes twinkling. "Your mother sent me to fetch you," he said. "The royal guests are starting to arrive."

"I didn't know they were coming so early!" Scarlett jumped up. She looked back at the ruby and the jewel-making tools as she left the room. She hoped there would be time to try out the tools before tonight's banquet.

❤️

Six carriages were lined up on the drive outside Bearbrook Castle. Servants were rushing everywhere, carrying suitcases and seeing to the horses. Two little princesses

were running around on the lawn, giggling.
"Bailey! Taylor!" called a queen with a
long purple cloak. "Don't get grass on your
dresses."

Queen Ruth was welcoming people on
the steps and she called Scarlett forward.
"Scarlett, come and meet King Thomas and
Queen Freda... This is Duke Robert... Say
hello to Queen Umasa..."

Scarlett curtsied and smiled at everyone.
It was amazing to see so many guests! She
would never remember everybody's names.

Her mum stopped beside a stocky man
with a beard. "I beg your pardon! Are
you...?"

"I'm King Bruno of Lidvia." The man
bowed deeply but didn't smile.

"Of course! Welcome to the Kingdom of
Deronda. It's been such a long time since
we last met and I think you've grown your
beard. I feel I hardly recognise you."

King Bruno bowed again and moved on.

A very young prince began tugging on his mum's sleeve and whining, "I'm hungry!"

"Let's all go inside and have a slice of strawberry cake," said Queen Ruth. "You can look after the older princesses, can't you, Scarlett? Get them something to eat and then show them the castle."

All the grown-ups drifted inside and Scarlett was left on the castle steps with two girls that looked the same age as her.

One princess had a pale-green dress and blonde hair that hung over her shoulders. She grinned at Scarlett, her blue eyes sparkling. The other princess was staring down at the steps, so that her long dark hair hid some of her face. She was wearing a long yellow dress tied around the waist with a ribbon.

Scarlett's heart skipped. She didn't meet other princesses very often, except for her

older cousin Ella. She hoped they would all become friends straightaway!

The blonde-haired girl spoke first. "Are you Scarlett? I can't wait for your birthday tomorrow!"

"Yes, I'm Scarlett," said Scarlett, smiling at them both. "Welcome to Bearbrook Castle!"

Chapter Two

The Baby River Otter

Scarlett showed the princesses where to hang up their cloaks. All the kings and queens were in the banquet hall, so she led the girls to the parlour and rang the bell for Mr Ellis, the butler. Mr Ellis brought in a cake topped with strawberries and vanilla icing. It looked so delicious Scarlett knew at once she was going to want more than one slice!

"So where do you come from?" she asked as she poured them each a glass of lemonade.

"My name's Lily." The girl in the green dress shook back her fair hair. "I live in Estaland, which is a very long way from here. We have some wonderful animals, like kangaroos, and parrots with rainbow-coloured wings."

"I love parrots but I've never seen a real one – only pictures in books," said Scarlett.

The other princess shyly tucked her dark hair behind her ear. "I'm Zina from the Kingdom of Ramova. My island is covered in tropical rainforests, and lemurs play in the treetops."

"I wish I could visit your kingdoms and see all the amazing wildlife!" said Scarlett. "I could show you some of the animals that live here if you like? There's always something to see down by the river."

"Yes, please!" Lily's blue eyes sparkled. "I love animals."

"Me too!" Zina smiled.

Scarlett led them back towards the castle entrance. There was a murmur of voices from the kings and queens in the banquet hall.

Queen Ruth waved as the girls passed the door, calling to Scarlett, "The banquet's at five o'clock. Make sure you're back in time."

Scarlett waved to her mum before heading across the garden, past the trampoline that she'd got for her birthday last year. "I always come this way." Scarlett stopped by the side entrance. "It's a lot quicker than going to the main gate."

The guard by the gate smiled and opened it for the princesses. Beyond the castle wall, the meadow gleamed in the sunshine. Golden buttercups and tall white daisies were scattered among a sea of waving grasses. Butterflies flitted from flower to flower, their wings shimmering as they moved.

"I think he likes me!" Lily giggled as a butterfly with orange-tipped wings settled on her fair hair.

Scarlett pushed her way through the tall grass to the path that ran beside the brook. Beyond the river lay a thick forest, and a tall mountain with a snowy peak rose up above the trees.

The water rushed along the stony riverbed, frothing and gurgling. On the opposite bank, two ducks were sleeping with their heads under their wings. A line of smooth, flat stepping stones led across the water.

"The river splits in two just up there and runs round on both sides, so this bit in the middle is an island. Come on – I'll take you across." Scarlett jumped on to the first stepping stone. "No one else ever comes here. I call it Bear Island because there's a rock that looks just like a bear in the middle."

Zina stopped by the edge, dipped her fingers in the water and shivered. "It's so cold! The rivers at home are much warmer."

"You get used to it," Scarlett told her. "I paddle a lot – especially in the summer." She sprang lightly across the stepping stones.

Zina followed, her dark hair swinging as she skipped across. A shy smile broke out on her face as she leapt on to the opposite bank.

Lily crossed more slowly, stopping on each stone to get her balance. She wobbled a lot but finally made it to the other side. "You're so lucky, Scarlett. Imagine having a secret island all to yourself!"

Scarlett grinned widely. She was used to exploring on her own. It was so nice to have two friends to share the place with. "Look – there's a squirrel." She pointed at a tree. "And there's a hare – it has very long ears."

The others watched as the little grey hare drank from the river before hopping back into the bushes.

"I'll show you my den!" Scarlett ran along a little path that was covered with twigs and pine needles. The wind made the pine trees sway and rustled the leaves of the beech trees.

"This is Bear Rock!" Scarlett patted the huge boulder that looked just like a bear rearing up on two legs. "And here's my den. Come inside!"

The three girls crowded into the little den, which was made from sticks and leaves. Scarlett found a packet of chocolate biscuits that she'd hidden in a hollow in the tree trunk and offered them round.

"This is amazing!" said Lily, munching her biscuit. "Do you ever see real bears?"

"Sometimes I see black bears but it's best to keep away from them, especially if they have cubs," Scarlett told her. "The den's fallen down a bit actually. I think the wind and rain have knocked some of the branches over."

"Maybe we could help you build it up again," said Zina.

They all agreed that this was a great idea so they spent a long time finding branches to add to the den, before putting leaves and moss over the roof. Then they went back to the river to wash the mud off their hands.

Scarlett took off her shoes and socks and waded into the shallows. Up ahead, there was a little pool below a sparkling waterfall. The river tumbled over a cliff, frothing and foaming at the bottom. "Come in if you want!" she called to the others. "It isn't deep at all."

Zina tiptoed in carefully, holding her yellow skirt in one hand.

Lily waded right in and stretched her hand under the waterfall, letting the water run over her fingers.

A whiskery face with two bright black

eyes peeped out of a hole in the opposite bank. The baby river otter watched the girls eagerly. Then he bounded out of his den, his stubby ears pricked up. Pausing at the edge of the water, he sniffed the air with his little round nose.

"Here's one of the baby otters," Scarlett whispered urgently. "There's a mother with four young living in that burrow and the babies only came out of the den for the first time last week. Don't splash – we don't want to scare him."

The princesses kept very still, watching in delight as the baby otter jumped in and out of the water, squeaking happily. Water drops glistened on his whiskers. Three more little otters sprang out of the burrow, followed by a much larger one.

"That must be their mother," whispered Lily. "Can the babies swim?"

Scarlett nodded. "They're all amazing

swimmers! Maybe if we go back to the riverbank they'll come in the water properly."

Quickly, the princesses waded to the edge and sat down on the sandy bank, letting their feet dry in the warm sunshine.

Just as Scarlett hoped, the otters leapt into the river. They swam gracefully, diving around each other and floating through the water reeds. The mother otter kept an eye on the girls but seemed to decide they weren't dangerous.

"They're lovely!" Zina tucked her dark hair behind her ear. "I never thought otters would make such funny squeaky noises."

Scarlett smiled. She was so pleased the otters had come out to play. "Sometimes I sit and watch them for ages. I think they've got quite used to me!"

"That little furry one is so cute." Lily pointed to the first baby otter.

"I call him Sparky because he's got so much energy," said Scarlett. "The first time I saw him..." She stopped suddenly. What was that strange buzzing sound?

The buzzing grew louder until it seemed to roar in her ears. A boat zoomed into view, churning up the surface of the river. Two men sat inside it – one with his hands on the wheel.

The mother otter barked in alarm. Scarlett jumped up, her heart racing. Boats didn't usually come along this part of the river – especially speed boats with noisy engines. She had to stop them before the little otters got hurt!

Chapter Three

The Dangerous Boat

Scarlett waved her arms at the boat. "Stop! There are otters in the river." But the boat was so loud, she could hardly hear herself speaking.

The boat raced past the girls at top speed. One of the men gave a shout, spotting the waterfall. He spun the wheel at the last moment, driving the boat into the bank and churning up the earth around the otter's den.

The otters scattered in all directions, darting out of the water and disappearing into the bushes.

The engine chugged to a stop and a man with grey hair jumped out, pulling the boat around. "Look what you did!" he snapped at the other man. "You could have made a hole in the boat driving into the bank like that."

"Well, I didn't know there was a waterfall here, did I?" The second man straightened his baseball cap.

"Excuse me!" called Scarlett. "Please don't turn your engine back on. You almost ran over a family of otters."

The men stared at the princesses. "How are we supposed to get back without using the engine?" scoffed the grey-haired man. "Who are you, anyway?"

Scarlett's cheeks grew red. These men were very rude. "I'm Princess Scarlett from Bearbrook Castle," she said. "Don't you have any oars? You could use those instead of the engine."

"You're a princess?" sneered the man in the baseball cap. "Princesses don't wade around in rivers getting their dresses muddy."

"Yes they do!" said Scarlett fiercely. "Princesses can do anything they like. We don't just sit around wearing tiaras."

The two men exchanged looks. "If they're telling the truth at least we know we're in the right place," said the grey-haired man, and his friend nodded. "We're going now, Your Highnesses." He bowed mockingly to the girls. "We'll just ... do our fishing a bit further down the river."

With a roar of the engine, they zoomed away, leaving the water foaming behind them.

"They should be ashamed of themselves!" stormed Scarlett. "Look at what they've done."

A large part of the river bank had been scraped away by the boat and the entrance to the otters' burrow was blocked.

"They were horrible," agreed Zina. "And if they were really fishing, why didn't they have any fishing rods? And what did they mean about being in the right place?"

Scarlett looked around worriedly. "Did you see where the otters went? I hope they're all right."

"I saw them jump out of the water and run into those bushes," Lily told her. "Maybe they'll come back when it's quiet."

"I hope so." Scarlett peered round the bramble patch that Lily had pointed to. She couldn't get rid of the feeling that something was wrong.

A little yelp came from the next bush along. Scarlett pushed the branches aside and there, hiding beneath the leaves, was Sparky – the smallest baby otter. He looked up at the girls with fearful black eyes.

"Poor little thing!" said Zina. "That boat really scared him."

Scarlett crouched down and held out her hand. "Sparky, are you all right?"

Sparky limped out of the bush and gave a sad yelp. He was holding one of his front paws against his furry tummy as if it was hurting.

"He's injured!" Zina crouched down too.

"Maybe the waves from the boat knocked him on to a rock," Lily suggested. "He needs his family but they've all run away."

"Let's find them!" said Scarlett. "Be careful though. We don't want to scare them all over again."

The princesses crept around the island, looking behind bushes and patches of reeds. Scarlett even checked inside her den but there was no sign of the otter family. She ran back to check on Sparky. "Maybe the otters were so scared that they ran a really long way," she said to the others.

Lily nodded. "That's what I'm afraid

of … and Sparky can't look after himself, especially with an injured leg."

"We can't stay here much longer though," said Zina quietly. "What time is the banquet?"

"Five o'clock." Scarlett glanced at the setting sun. Time had flown by while they were playing in the den and now it was getting late. Sparky nudged her hand with his nose and gave a soft little squeak.

Scarlett knew she couldn't leave Sparky alone on the riverbank. "Let's take him back to the castle with us. We can feed him and keep him warm. Then tomorrow we can come back and look for his family again." She smiled. "That's exactly what a Rescue Princess would do!"

"What's a Rescue Princess?" Lily asked eagerly.

Scarlett gently picked up Sparky. His brown fur was soft against her arms. "I'll tell you all about it on the way. We'd better hurry!"

The princesses went back to the stepping stones and crossed the river. The setting sun shone over the meadow, turning the tall grass golden.

Scarlett explained to Lily and Zina everything she knew about being a Rescue Princess. She told them about her cousin's adventures and how Ella had sent her some jewel-making tools for her birthday.

"Magic jewels!" Lily's blue eyes widened. "Have you made any yet?"

"No, I only opened the parcel just before you arrived," said Scarlett. "But I really want to make one soon!"

"It all sounds so exciting!" said Lily.

Zina nodded eagerly. "And helping animals is really important."

Scarlett knocked on the castle gate. She was a little worried about what the guard would say when he saw the otter, but he was too busy talking to another guard to notice. Sparky wriggled in her arms as they crossed the garden and climbed the castle steps. Scarlett held him tighter. Her arms were really starting to ache.

"Here – I can help you!" Zina ran inside and pulled her cloak down from the coat peg. Then she took the little otter from Scarlett, wrapping him up in the cloak so that only his face was showing.

"Your Royal Highnesses!" Mr Ellis, the butler, came into the hallway and bowed.

"Queen Ruth asked me to remind you that the banquet begins in fifteen minutes."

Scarlett sprang in front of Zina, blocking the butler's view of the baby otter. "Thank you, Mr Ellis. We'll go and get ready straightaway."

Zina blushed. "Did he notice anything?" she whispered when the butler had gone.

"I don't think so," said Lily, giggling.

"Mr Ellis hates mess." Scarlett warned them as they climbed the stairs. "If he'd noticed Sparky he might have told us to leave him outside." She pointed to some suitcases in the corridor. "Look, your cases have been brought up. I'm glad your rooms are in the tower next to mine."

They went into Scarlett's bedroom and Zina sat down on the bed with Sparky. Lily rushed straight over to the jewel-making tools, which Scarlett had left on her dressing table, and picked up each one in turn.

Crouching down, Scarlett looked at Sparky's injured paw. "There's a thorn in it! That must be why it's hurting." Gently, she pulled out the spiky thorn. "There you go! Now we just need to find you somewhere to rest." She took a toy box and tipped all the teddies on to the floor, before filling it with woolly jumpers.

Zina carefully lay Sparky on the jumpers and stroked his furry tummy. The little otter sniffed at his new home before curling up and closing his eyes. "What do otters eat?" she asked suddenly. "Maybe we can save him some of our dinner."

"They like fish a lot," began Scarlett, but she was cut short by a loud clanging noise from downstairs. "That's the dinner bell. We'd better hurry!"

Lily and Zina dashed to their rooms. Scarlett glanced in the mirror. Her dress was still damp in places, with mud along the hem, and her shoes were wet too. Her parents would be disappointed if she didn't look smart for the royal banquet.

She changed into a dark-green dress edged with velvet ribbon. Then she brushed her curly dark hair at lightning speed, before putting on the sparkling emerald tiara that matched her dress. Slipping her feet into some green shoes, she dashed out into the hallway.

"I'm ready!" Lily ran down the corridor holding a silver tiara on top of her fair hair. Her blue dress swirled round her legs. "I got changed really fast."

Zina hurried out of her room wearing a white dress and carrying a tiara dotted with diamonds. "I'm here! Can someone help me put this on? It's so fiddly."

Scarlett took the diamond tiara and pinned it into Zina's hair. "There – you look great!" She took one last look at Sparky. He was asleep on his back with his paws curled

over. His eyes were shut and his pale tummy rose and fell peacefully. "I don't like to leave him by himself, but at least he's asleep so he won't miss us."

The dinner bell started up again, making the girls jump.

"Quickly! We must be really late – they never ring it twice." Scarlett dashed down the winding stairs.

Lily and Zina rushed after her, their skirts floating out behind them. Scarlett skidded to a halt outside the banquet hall and tried to catch her breath before walking in. The hall was lit by large golden lamps. The long dining table was set with rows of sparkling glasses and white plates with golden edges.

The kings, queens, lords and ladies all turned to look at the princesses and Scarlett felt herself blushing. "Sorry we're late." She curtsied. "We were just talking upstairs."

"Don't worry! We haven't started yet."

Her father, King Philip, smiled broadly.
"Come and sit down. Did you show the other princesses the meadow by the river, Scarlett? It's so pretty at this time of year."

"Yes, it was really warm and sunny outside." Scarlett hurried over to the empty seats at the far end of the table. She was two seats along from the king with the beard – King Bruno from Lidvia – and she saw him glance darkly in her direction. Maybe he really hated people being late to dinner.

A moment later the butler came round with bowls of chicken soup and soft buttered rolls. Harry, the young prince, spilled soup on his shirt and Queen Ruth hurried to find him another napkin.

"That was lovely!" Scarlett put down her spoon. "I bet the next course will be great too! Is it fish?"

Lily and Zina giggled. They knew exactly why Scarlett was asking about the next

course. Fish would be perfect to take to
Sparky!

"Actually we're having roast beef," said
King Philip. "And we have cheesecake or
chocolate ice cream sundaes for dessert."

Scarlett's face dropped. "Oh! That sounds
nice, I guess."

The banquet carried on and Scarlett tried
to wait patiently as each course came and
went. At last, everyone had finished dessert
and the grown-ups went to the parlour to
drink coffee.

The princesses curtsied and said
goodnight. When they were out of sight,
Scarlett led the others towards the kitchen.
"We'll have to search for some fish. Sparky
will be hungry by now."

"Are you sure your parents won't mind?"
asked Zina.

"They've always told me that animals
should be properly looked after," said Scarlett.

"The only thing is our cook, Mrs Linny, doesn't like people coming into her kitchen. We'll have to try not to be seen."

Lily nodded. "Don't worry – we're right behind you!"

Scarlett crept down the passage, stopping in the kitchen doorway. Her heart beat faster. This was her first chance to try some ninja moves, just like in Ella's stories about the Rescue Princesses!

On the right was the refrigerator where the fish was kept, but Mrs Linny was washing up at the sink and more servants could come back at any moment.

"You go!" Lily whispered in Scarlett's ear. "I'll distract her."

Scarlett sneaked inside, keeping as low as she could. On tiptoes, she crept behind a worktop.

"Excuse me!" Lily said loudly. "Are you the cook? I just wanted to thank you for the

delicious meal we had tonight."

Scarlett opened the refrigerator door as quietly as she could. On the top shelf was a pack of white fish. She grabbed it and tucked it under her arm. Lily finished thanking the cook and the princesses hurried away again.

"That was quick thinking," Scarlett told Lily, as they ran up the spiral stairs.

"Thanks!" Lily wrinkled her nose. "Wow, that fish smells strong!"

Scarlett laughed. "I'm sure Sparky won't mind about that! I wonder if he's still sleeping." She pushed her bedroom door and it swung open before she'd even turned the handle. Hadn't she closed it properly?

"Sparky?" Zina called. "Are you awake?"

Scarlett hurried across the room and looked into the box where they'd left the little otter. Her stomach twisted. The toy box was empty and Sparky was gone.

Chapter Five

Sparky's Adventure

Scarlett rummaged in the box, desperately hoping that the little otter was underneath the jumpers, but there was nothing there. "He's gone! What shall we do?"

"Maybe he'll come out if he smells food." Lily took the fish parcel and undid the paper. "Sparky! We've got something for you."

Scarlett gazed around, hoping to see a cute little face peeping out with bright eyes, a round black nose and whiskers. Crouching down, she looked under the bed, behind the wardrobe and under her dressing table.

Lily and Zina began searching too. Zina lifted up the bedcovers, while Lily looked under the pile of cuddly toys lying on the floor. There was still no sign of Sparky.

"We should check along the corridor," said Scarlett. "Oh, I wish I'd shut the door properly!"

Zina bit her lip. "He might have gone to explore and got lost. I hope he's not frightened."

Scarlett ran out into the passage. The castle was huge. How would they ever find the baby otter? "Quick, we have to start searching!"

The three girls hurried down the corridor, looking in every corner. Scarlett even opened the laundry basket to peer inside. Luckily, most of the doors along the corridor were shut.

"I don't think we need to check those." Lily pointed to a row of closed doors. "Otters can't

reach door handles."

Finding no sign of Sparky, they hurried down to the floor below. The sound of voices drifted up from the parlour. Scarlett heard her parents' voices among them. Her heart raced. She knew most of the royal guests had rooms on this floor. She hoped the grown-ups didn't decide to go to bed early!

There were more rooms to check this time and many of the visitors had left their doors ajar. To save time, the girls worked out a quick way to test whether the otter was in each room. Lily would open the door and Zina would call Sparky's name, while Scarlett wafted the fish around in the air. Then they would wait a few seconds and listen for rustlings and squeaks.

They checked ten rooms like this, but when they reached the eleventh there were noises inside.

"This is my parents' room and my dad

often has a bath after dinner," Scarlett told the others. "I think I can hear the water running – wait for me here!"

She knocked on the door before going in. There were sounds coming from the bathroom. Scarlett knew that Mr Ellis, the butler, usually ran the bath for the king. Then he would turn off the taps and tell her dad that the bath was ready.

Scarlett began to back away. She didn't want the butler to find her searching the room and ask her what she was up to.

Splish-splash! Splish-splash!

Scarlett froze. Why was Mr Ellis making those splashing noises? What was he doing?

Lily opened the door and whispered, "Scarlett, we have to hurry! The butler's coming up the stairs."

"Really! I thought he was in here." Scarlett looked over the bannister and spotted Mr Ellis carrying a pile of towels.

Splish-splash! The noise came again. If Mr Ellis wasn't making the sound and her dad was still downstairs, then who was in there?

Putting a finger to her lips, Scarlett beckoned Lily and Zina into her parents' room. Together they crept towards the bathroom and peered around the door.

Sparky was paddling up and down the bath and diving under the water cascading from the taps as if it was a little waterfall. He climbed up the side of the bath and sniffed at the king's lavender soap and crown-shaped sponge before jumping right back in with a splash. He squeaked when he saw the girls and shook the water from his whiskers.

Scarlett smiled, kneeling down beside the bath. "Sparky, what are you doing? We've been looking for you everywhere."

"He must have followed the sound of running water," said Lily.

"He loves it in there." Zina smiled.

"We can run a bath for him upstairs instead. We have to get him out of here before Mr Ellis comes back." Scarlett pictured how the butler would look if he saw a river otter in the king's bath. He would probably call for the guards! "Come here, Sparky." She tried to lift the baby otter out of the water but Sparky squeaked naughtily and slipped out of her hands.

"Use the fish!" hissed Zina. "I'll distract the butler."

Lily turned off the taps while Scarlett held the smelly fish above the water. Sparky stopped paddling, his whiskers twitching. "Come on – this way!" Scarlett coaxed, edging towards the bathroom door.

"Sorry to bother you!" Zina's voice floated in from the corridor. "I think I forgot to pack my toothpaste. Do you have any spare?"

"Yes, I think so," the butler replied. "I'll just turn off the bath taps and then I'll—"

"It's all right, Mr Ellis, I've turned them off already." Scarlett hid the fish behind her back and poked her head around the door. "I heard the bath running and I didn't want it to get too full."

"Right! Well, actually I *never* let it get too full." Mr Ellis frowned. "But thank you anyway. I'll find you that toothpaste now, Your Highness."

"Oh, thank you!" Scarlett heard Zina say. There was a pause before she whispered. "It's all right – the butler's gone!"

Scarlett felt Sparky's wet fur brush against her ankles. The little otter jumped up, trying to reach the fish. Then he shook his fur, splattering water everywhere. Lily giggled and tried to catch the baby otter but he slipped through her fingers.

Scarlet knelt down and gave Sparky the fish before scooping him up into her arms. The baby otter lay there happily,

gobbling his food.

"It's lucky we found you before Mr Ellis did," she told him, laughing. "I think you enjoyed your castle adventure!"

Chapter Six

Scarlett's Ruby

Scarlett crept back to her bedroom, holding Sparky tightly. Zina helped to dry him with a towel and they settled him down on the jumpers in the toy box again.

When the baby otter had fallen asleep, Scarlett went to the kitchen to fetch three mugs of hot chocolate, which she carried upstairs on a tray. The princesses sipped their drinks and talked about how they planned to search for the otter family in the morning.

"Tell us some more about the Rescue Princesses, Scarlett!" said Lily. "It sounds so exciting. Are there really princesses who help animals in trouble?"

"Yes, my cousin Ella joined them after starting school at the Royal Academy for Princesses. She began by saving a little lost rabbit." Scarlett took out Ella's letters, which she kept in a drawer. "But if I tell you any more, you have to promise to keep it a secret. Ella says only girls who really love animals are allowed to join the Rescue Princesses."

Lily and Zina gazed back with solemn faces. "We promise not to tell," they said.

"And we REALLY love animals!" added Zina.

Scarlett smiled and unfolded one of the letters. "Ella tells me all about their adventures. This one began with a naughty bunny called Daisy and a secret passageway inside the castle..." She read out the letter, enjoying her friends' spellbound faces.

"What other animals have they helped?"
Lily asked eagerly after Scarlett had finished.

Scarlett looked through the letters. "The
first one was a little baby deer – that's when
the Rescue Princesses was invented. Since
then they've rescued dolphins, lion cubs,
pandas and snow leopards as well as a kitten
and a puppy! They've had lots of adventures
in different lands and more princesses have
joined along the way."

"And what about the ninja moves?" asked
Zina. "They sound awesome."

Scarlett turned over more pages. "Ella
hasn't told me very much about them
but we could probably make up our own
ninja moves. It's all about making sure the
baddies don't see you."

"We're already really close to being Rescue
Princesses!" said Lily happily. "We're looking
after Sparky."

"All we need now are some magic jewels

to help us." Scarlett sat down at her dressing table and touched the smooth, oval-shaped ruby. The jewel gleamed a beautiful, warm red colour. She had been ready to try shaping it with the jewel-making tools this morning before the royal visitors had arrived. So much had happened since then!

Lily and Zina crowded round her.

"Go on, Scarlett," urged Lily. "Let's see what happens!"

Scarlett picked up Ella's latest letter and read the part about the jewels again. "*The jewels must be shaped perfectly to release the magic*," she read out loud. Turning the paper over, she studied the picture drawn by Jaminta, the jewel expert, on the back.

"Try that one." Lily pointed to the drawing of an eight-sided jewel. "That looks brilliant!"

"All right – I'll have a go!" Scarlett's stomach fluttered nervously as she picked up

a chisel and the tiny silver hammer.
She put the chisel against the ruby and
then tapped the end of it with the hammer.
A little flake of the ruby broke off. Scarlett
turned the jewel around and tried again.
She kept on chipping away until the ruby
became a pretty octagon shape with eight
smooth sides.

"That looks lovely!" Zina told her.

"But has it worked?" asked Lily.

"I don't know." Scarlett frowned and laid
down the tools. She picked up the ruby and
looked at it closely. The jewel didn't seem
any more magical than before.

Lily took it from her and gave the ruby a
shake. "Nothing's happening! What kind of
magic is it meant to have?"

"I'm not sure." Scarlett looked at Ella's
letter again. "My cousin says you won't
know until something happens. One girl
invented some rings with jewels that let the

Rescue Princesses talk to each other when they were far apart. I think those would be really handy."

"Rings that let you talk to each other?" Lily looked doubtful.

"Yes, you just press the jewel to make it work," explained Scarlett.

Lily squeezed the ruby but nothing happened. She handed the gem back. "But have you actually *seen* any of these magic jewels? Because maybe it's just a story."

"Ella's seen some of them." Scarlett looked at Lily in surprise. "So I know it's true."

Lily gave a little shrug, then she yawned. "Well, I'm going back to my room. I want to take off this itchy dress and put my pyjamas on. See you in the morning!"

The door swung shut and Scarlett looked at Zina. "She doesn't believe me about the jewels." She put the ruby down, trying to swallow her disappointment.

"Maybe I'm not using the tools right, but I'm sure I copied Jaminta's drawing properly."

"We don't really need anything magical right now," said Zina. "Sparky's safe and tomorrow we can take him to find his family."

"You're right!" Scarlett cheered up. "It's helping Sparky that's important."

After Zina left, Scarlett watched Sparky sleeping. He looked so sweet curled up in the jumpers! She was determined to look after him and make sure he got back to the river safely the next day.

She glanced at her clock. It was really late but she wanted a drink of water. Putting on her pink and white pyjamas, Scarlett crept downstairs. The lights were off which meant that everyone had gone to bed.

On her way back from the kitchen, she noticed someone walking around the banquet hall holding a torch. It was King Bruno, rubbing his beard and muttering to himself.

Scarlett peered round the door. There was something a bit strange about King Bruno. At least this gave her a chance to try out her ninja moves so that he didn't see her. Keeping to the shadows, she tiptoed past the doorway. Then she sprang up the stairs avoiding the third step, which always made a loud creak.

Ninja moves were about making sure she wasn't seen or heard, she told herself. If King Bruno was going to sneak around the castle then she'd need to practise her Rescue Princess ninja moves as hard as she could!

Chapter Seven

The Great Otter Hunt

Scarlett woke up the next morning to find a warm furry shape cuddled up next to her on the blanket. Sparky must have climbed up on to her bed during the night. She sat up and the baby otter opened his eyes and yawned.

"Sparky!" Scarlett gently tickled his soft tummy. "I hope you slept all right?"

The little otter jumped down from the bed and started wrestling with a furry teddy that was lying on the floor. Scarlett smiled. He didn't seem to be missing his family too badly.

All the same, she knew she needed to get him back to the river. He would get hungry again soon and she couldn't take fish from the castle kitchen forever.

Her gaze fell on the ruby and the jewel-making tools on her dressing table. Suddenly, she remembered there were TWO reasons she was excited this morning. Sparky was here in the castle AND it was her birthday!

"I'm nine today!" she told Sparky, and the little otter twitched his whiskers as if he understood.

Quickly, Scarlett pulled on her favourite red dress. Then she turned on the taps and let some water run into the bath so that Sparky would have something to do while she was downstairs having breakfast.

The banquet hall was decorated with shiny streamers and a long golden banner that read *Happy Birthday Scarlett* hung above the

fireplace. Many of the royal visitors were already eating breakfast and they called out "Happy Birthday!" as Scarlett came in. Lily and Zina waved at her eagerly from the far end of the table.

Her mum hugged her, smiling. "Happy birthday! Are you excited?"

"VERY excited!" Scarlett beamed. "I love the decorations."

Mr Ellis coughed. "Many happy returns, Princess Scarlett. Would you like something special for your birthday breakfast?"

"Ooh, pancakes, please." Scarlett noticed Lily's eyes light up at the mention of pancakes. "And could the other princesses have some too?"

"Of course," said the butler. "I shall talk to Cook."

Soon the three princesses were tucking into stacks of pancakes topped with maple syrup and chocolate sprinkles.

"Did you sleep well, King Bruno?" asked Queen Ruth as the king with the fuzzy beard joined them at the breakfast table.

"I suppose so." King Bruno frowned. "But my room smelled terrible."

Some of the other guests nodded. "My room had a dreadful odour too!" said a queen in a purple hat. "It reminded me of fish."

"Oh dear!" Queen Ruth wrinkled her brow. "I'm not sure why. I'll ask Mr Ellis to air the rooms today."

Scarlett looked at Lily and Zina and stifled her giggles. Together they'd wafted a fish around the rooms when they were looking for Sparky. No wonder they'd left a funny smell!

After breakfast, Scarlett opened two birthday presents from her parents – a butterfly kite and an ice-cream making machine. "Thank you!" She hugged them. "Could I open my other presents later?

It's just I've promised to take Lily and Zina to the meadow again – we had so much fun there yesterday."

"All right then!" agreed Queen Ruth. "But don't forget we're having a special birthday lunch in the garden and then some party games."

The princesses changed into tops and leggings, which would be easy to roll up if they went paddling again. Scarlett popped Sparky in a rucksack and carried him carefully downstairs to where the other girls were waiting.

Bees buzzed around the flowers in the royal garden. The day was warm and even the castle's grey towers looked bright in the sunshine. As they crossed the garden, the baby otter wriggled and squeaked, and poked his whiskery nose out of the top of the bag.

"Do you think he's uncomfortable?" asked Zina anxiously.

"I'll get him out – no one's around."
Scarlett lifted up the little otter, planning to
carry him in her arms, but Sparky leapt out
of her hands and scampered away across
the palace lawn.

"Sparky, come back!" Lily ran after him.

The baby otter stopped to sniff the air
before galloping off again. He jumped over a
patch of daisies and hid behind a tree.

The princesses dashed after him, giggling.
Scarlett dived on to the grass but Sparky
slipped through her hands again.

"Oh no!" gasped Zina. "What shall we do?
We don't have any fish this time."

Scarlett grabbed a ball that was lying
behind a bush. "I think he just wants to
play." She threw the ball. "Here, Sparky!"

The otter's ears pricked up and he leapt
after the ball. Stopping it with his nose,
he squeaked happily. Lily picked up the
ball and threw it again. Soon they were all

playing ball-chase with the little otter and
giggling as he raced up and down.

When Sparky grew tired, Scarlett picked
him up again. The princesses went through
the side gate and headed across the
meadow. When they reached the river's edge
Sparky sniffed the air, his whiskers twitching.
Scarlett set him down on the bank and he
jumped straight into the water, but after
a minute he darted out again. He looked
around, as if confused, and his ears drooped.

Scarlett knelt down and stroked his soft
fur. "Are you wondering where your family
is? Don't worry, Sparky. We'll help you find
them."

"I think I can see them." Lily leapt on to
the stepping stones that spanned the river.
"They're over here!"

They crossed the water with Sparky
running at their heels. Dashing into the
bushes, Lily stopped suddenly. A squirrel

chattered at her before running up the trunk of a tree. "Oh! It wasn't an otter at all."

"Maybe one of us should stay here with Sparky while the others start searching?" suggested Zina. "I don't mind being the one that stays."

So Zina sat on the bank and amused the little otter by splashing in the shallows, while the others spread out to look around the island. Scarlett crept up to the otters' burrow and listened carefully at the entrance. There was no noise from inside and earth still blocked the mouth of the den. She pushed the soil aside, clearing the way into the burrow.

"Scarlett?" called Lily, from further along the bank. "I can see the otters! They're just down the river, swimming by the water reeds."

Scarlett's heart skipped a beat. "I'm coming!" She pulled off her shoes and jumped into the river.

Sparky squeaked with delight when he saw his family gliding and diving through the reeds. He paddled over to his mother and touched noses with her. Then he played with the other baby otters, splashing through the water and diving beneath the surface.

"Look how happy he is!" Scarlett cupped her hands to call back to Lily. "Thanks, Lily! They're all back together now."

Lily called back but her words were brushed away by the wind.

Scarlett turned to watch the otters again until Zina nudged her, saying, "Why isn't she coming back?"

"I don't know." Scarlett gazed up at Lily, who was standing on top of a rise in the riverbank. She seemed to be staring down the river.

"Lily, come down!" said Scarlett. "Everything's all right now."

Lily called out a third time and Scarlett finally caught the words. "She says there's a boat and it's coming in fast!"

The girls listened. A faint humming noise in the distance grew steadily louder.

"Oh no!" cried Zina. "I bet it's those men we saw yesterday."

Scarlett's eyes flashed. "Well, this time we're not going to let them scare the baby otters!"

Chapter Eight

Trouble at Bearbrook Castle

Scarlett and Zina waded out of the water and raced barefoot along the riverbank. Suddenly the boat roared around a bend in the river. It was the one they'd seen the day before with the same men – one with grey hair and the other in a baseball cap.

"Stop!" Scarlett waved her arms. "You'll run into the otters."

"Oh, it's the princesses again!" The grey-haired man gave a nasty smirk. "No need to worry. We'll turn off the engine

– we don't need it any more." He pointed to some oars before turning off the ear-splitting engine.

"Thank you," said Scarlett, "but it would be better if you didn't go any further. You're very close to the otters and their burrow."

The man's face darkened. "We'll go where we want. We're only here to do a bit of fishing." He turned away and began rowing with the oars. The boat glided smoothly past.

"What's happening?" Lily ran up, panting.

"They say they're just fishing but I don't trust them," whispered Zina. "Don't you think there's something funny about them?"

The grey-haired man kept rowing and the boat slid upstream. The princesses followed, watching as the men pulled the boat to the bank before getting out their fishing rods. The mother otter barked sharply to her young and she and the babies swam away towards the pool by the waterfall.

"I wish we didn't have to leave Sparky," sighed Scarlett. "At least the otters are all safe and those men have switched their engine off."

"When we get back to the castle you can open your other birthday presents," Zina reminded her.

"I can't wait till you see what my gift is!" said Lily.

Scarlett smiled. It was nice of the others to be excited about her birthday. She couldn't wait to open the rest of her presents, but at the same time she was worried about the men with the boat. What if they switched on the engine again? She cast one last look at the two men with their fishing rods before following her friends across the meadow.

❤️

When they reached the castle garden, Scarlett looked around in surprise. Where was everybody and where were the tables for her birthday lunch? She hurried up the castle steps just as Mr Ellis rushed past. "Is it nearly time for lunch, Mr Ellis? We could help you get things ready."

"I'm sorry, Princess Scarlett, but I can't fetch lunch just now. Some of the guests' valuables have been taken and the king is asking for the guards." The butler hurried away.

"Valuables!" Zina looked worried. "What does he mean?"

King Philip came out of the parlour, his crown lopsided. "Scarlett, have you seen a diamond bracelet or a necklace with a golden letter F? Queen Freda's jewellery has gone missing. King Thomas thinks his watch has disappeared too."

Scarlett noticed a lady sitting in the

parlour and dabbing her eyes with a hankerchief. It had to be Queen Freda. "No, I haven't seen anything like that. Did they lose the jewellery?"

Her dad looked serious. "No, I don't think so. They're quite certain they left their things safely in their rooms. I'm afraid someone may have stolen them." He marched away, calling for the guards.

"That's terrible!" Lily looked shocked.

"Maybe it's all a mistake," said Zina.

"But how would jewellery go missing by mistake?" demanded Scarlett, and the others shook their heads.

Scarlett climbed the stairs, thinking hard. Who would do something as awful as going into people's rooms and taking their things? She opened her bedroom door and stopped in the doorway, frowning.

"What it is, Scarlett?" asked Lily.

"I thought I left the ruby on my dressing

table." Scarlett stared at the row of silver chisels. "The tools are still here but the ruby's gone."

"Maybe it rolled on to the floor." Zina crouched down to look under the table.

Scarlett and Lily began to search too. They looked under the bed and behind the wardrobe. They even checked Scarlett's sock drawer but none of them could find it.

"Do you think whoever stole Queen Freda's jewellery took your ruby as well?" Zina's eyes were wide.

"Maybe." Scarlett opened her jewellery drawer. "It looks like my emerald tiara is missing too." Her heart sank. That tiara was her favourite.

"That's strange!" Lily was staring out of the window. "It's that king with the bushy beard – what's his name?"

"You mean King Bruno?" Scarlett went to the window. "I can't see him."

"There, by the wall." Lily pointed. "He looks like he's waiting for something."

The window gave a really good view of the garden and the meadow beyond. Far below, King Bruno was standing by the castle wall clutching a rucksack. He looked around as if checking that no one else was nearby. A guard came marching up the path and the king ducked behind a bush.

"What's he doing?" said Scarlett. "He's acting very suspiciously."

The two men from the boat ran across the meadow, stopping on the other side of the wall. Scarlett opened the window and the girls leaned forward to watch.

One of the men shouted something, but the girls were too far away to make out the words. Then, with a swing of his arm, King Bruno threw the rucksack into the air and it sailed right over the high castle wall. The two men ran to pick it up while King Bruno

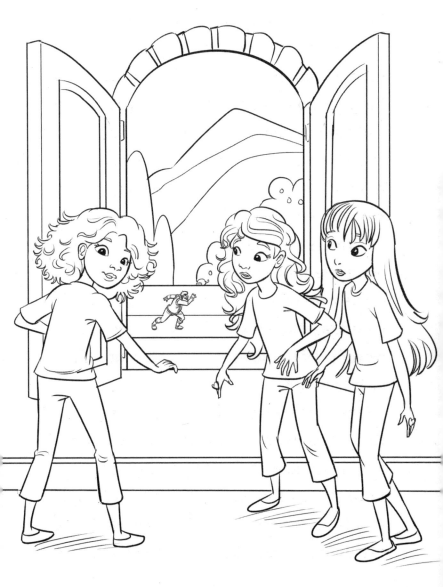

hurried back towards the castle.

Scarlett's heart sank. "I think the missing jewellery must be in that bag! King Bruno must have stolen everything and now he's given it to those men. The nasty, sneaky thief!"

"They must have been planning this all along," said Lily. "I *knew* those men weren't really here to catch fish."

"They'll try to get away fast in their boat. They might hurt the otters as they leave!" Zina's face creased with worry.

Scarlett's mind was whirling. "We won't let them. We'll send the guards after them before they get away!"

Chapter Nine

Leaping Ninjas

Scarlett rushed down the spiral stairs and the other princesses raced after her. A grey-haired queen, who was coming the other way, tutted as they dashed past. "In *my* day, we weren't allowed to run around in leggings. We had to wear a long dress and a crown at all times!"

Skidding to a halt in the parlour, Scarlett gazed round the empty room. Where was her dad and all the guards? Her friends crowded in behind her.

"Scarlett, look!" whispered Lily, nodding

toward the window.

The room wasn't empty after all. Queen Freda was sitting in an armchair with a hankerchief in her hand.

Scarlett dropped a curtsy. "I'm so sorry your things have gone missing, Queen Freda. I think I know who took them – have you seen my parents?"

"It's all right, my dear." Queen Freda managed a weak smile. "King Bruno told them all about the thieves that drove away in the carriage. The guards saddled their horses and galloped down the road, and your parents have gone with them. They all left a few minutes ago. I just hope they catch those wicked robbers before they get too far."

Scarlett's stomach lurched. "King Bruno told them about some thieves who had a carriage ... and they believed him?"

"Of course they did," said Queen Freda. "There's no need for you to worry. Now, go and play like a good girl!"

Scarlett turned to Lily and Zina. "King Bruno tricked them!" she whispered. "And now the guards are gone so we have to stop those men ourselves... I think it's time for some ninja moves!"

The princesses crept to the castle door and scanned the garden carefully. There were no guards anywhere but King Bruno was standing at the end of the drive beside the main gate.

"Do you think he's making sure no one follows those men to the boat?" asked Zina.

"Maybe," said Lily. "We have to reach the side gate without him spotting us."

"We can do it!" Scarlett's eyes gleamed. "Just keep really low and use all the hiding places you can." She waited till King Bruno had turned away, before dashing down the steps and jumping behind a fir tree.

One by one, the girls darted behind trees and statues, stopping to check if King Bruno was looking. When they reached the castle wall, there were no guards and the side gate was firmly locked.

"What do we do now?" Lily gazed up at the smooth wooden gate. "Is there a spare key somewhere?"

Scarlett shook her head. "I don't think so. And we can't climb over it – the sides are too smooth."

"Then we're stuck ... unless we can jump as high as a kangaroo," said Lily.

An idea popped into Scarlett's head. "That's it! We can jump over. Zina, I need as many cushions as you can find. Lily, I need your help with the trampoline."

Zina ran back to the castle while Scarlett and Lily raced over to the trampoline. It took all their strength to pull it across the grass. Scarlett darted a look at King Bruno. What would he do if he saw them? Luckily there was a thick patch of bushes blocking his view

of the side gate.

At last, Scarlett and Lily managed to push the trampoline right up against the wooden gate. When Zina came back with armfuls of cushions, Scarlett climbed on to the trampoline and threw them over the top one by one. She couldn't see over the other side to check where the cushions had fallen but she'd thrown them as carefully as she could.

"I think I should go first. I don't want either of you getting hurt if this doesn't work." Scarlett's heart pounded as she got into the centre of the trampoline. She would have to jump higher than she'd ever jumped before!

She bounced lightly, soaring higher with each spring. Then she made the most enormous leap, tucking her legs into her tummy. She held her breath as she zoomed upwards.

"Go, Scarlett!" cheered Zina and Lily.

Scarlett brushed the top of the gate with her toes and plunged down the other side, landing on the soft cushions on her hands and knees. Her stomach felt wobbly but she'd made it! "I'm all right," she called. "It worked!"

Scarlett quickly put the scattered cushions back into position. She could hear whispers on the other side of the gate. Then at last Lily's head appeared, bobbing up and down as she jumped on the trampoline. "It's no good! I'm never going to get over," she cried. "You should all go without me."

"We can't do that!" Scarlett called softly. "Rescue Princesses have to stick together!"

Lily stopped bouncing, then she tried again. This time she tucked her knees in tight enough to jump right over the gate. She landed and scrambled up, beaming. "I did it! I never thought I would."

Zina came last, leaping gracefully over the gate. Then the girls hid the cushions behind a bush before running across the meadow.

Scarlett ducked behind the long grass as soon as she saw the men.

A bucket half full of fish stood on the seat of the boat beside a pair fishing rods. The grey-haired man was pushing the boat into the middle of the river. The other man was looking inside King Bruno's rucksack. Scarlett caught a gleam of gold and diamonds before he shut the bag.

"Let's get out of here," said the grey-haired man. "We've already wasted enough time catching these fish!"

As the other man laughed, Scarlett saw the water ripple by the side of the boat. A little black nose with whiskers poked out of the water. Then a baby otter scrambled over the side of the boat, scampering towards the bucket of fish.

Scarlett's heart froze. It was Sparky! "Oh no! What are we going to do?"

The others had spotted him too. "Stop

it, Sparky!" hissed Zina. "Come away from there."

The otter didn't hear them. Standing on his hind legs, he poked his head into the fish bucket.

The grey-haired man saw him. "Hey! Get out of there, you little pest!"

Sparky's whiskers quivered and he shrank back, hiding behind the bucket.

"We have to help him!" Scarlett sprang out of her hiding place and together the girls pelted towards the riverbank.

"Not you again!" The older man jumped aboard as soon as he saw them, yelling to his friend, "Start the engine!"

The engine roared and the boat zoomed off, churning the water into foam. Scarlett caught one last glimpse of Sparky trembling behind the fish bucket as they sped away. Then they vanished round the bend in the river, taking the baby otter with them.

Chapter Ten

Crossing Bear Island

Scarlett stared after the boat, her heart thumping. She couldn't stop picturing Sparky, cowering behind the bucket of fish. He'd looked so scared.

"Quick – we have to catch them!" cried Zina.

Scarlett thought quickly. "There's a short cut over Bear Island but it's really tricky crossing the river on the other side." She saw the determined looks on her friends' faces. "All right – I'll show you!" She led them to the stepping stones that spanned the river.

The princesses followed the straightest path across the middle of the island. Brambles snagged their leggings and low-hanging branches caught against their hair. The undergrowth rustled as birds, squirrels and mice scampered away from their running feet. At last Scarlett spotted the steep bank that bordered this part of the island.

The river gurgled at the bottom of a rocky ravine. Trees grew right up to the cliff edge and one oak tree branch stretched over the river like a long arm.

"The water's too deep to wade across just here," Scarlett told them. "But the river's narrow and if we use this branch we should be able to climb along and jump to the other side." She leaned on the branch with both hands to check that it felt strong.

"Maybe we should go one at a time," said Lily nervously.

Zina went first, sitting on the branch and pushing herself along. Reaching the end, she leapt off and landed on the sandy bank.

Scarlett noticed that Lily had turned pale. "Why don't you go next? I'll hold the branch steady for you."

"Thanks!" Climbing up, Lily pushed her way to the end. Her hands clenched tightly around the branch. "I don't like being high up. I don't think I can do this!"

Scarlett clambered up to join her, ignoring the sharp creaking of the tree. "Hold my hand and we'll jump together!"

Lily took her hand and held tight. Scarlett leapt off the branch, pulling her friend along with her. For one long moment it felt like they were flying. The water bubbled over the rocky riverbed below. The wind rushed past and Scarlett's dark curls fluttered. A second later, they splashed into the water right at the edge of the river.

Zina leaned down and pulled them out of the shallows.

"We did it!" Lily gasped. "That was scary though."

"That was the hard bit!" Scarlett scrambled up the bank. "Now we can catch up with the boat. See how the river doubles back on itself over there?" She paused, frowning. "We should hear the boat engine. Where are they?"

Running to the brow of the next hill, the girls scanned the river.

"Over there!" panted Zina. "You can see the boat through the trees. But why has it stopped moving?"

"Maybe they think they're safe and they're looking through the stolen jewels again," said Lily.

"Maybe Sparky managed to jump off." Scarlett crossed her fingers, hoping it was true.

They ran down the slope to a cluster of fir trees and peered through the spiky leaves. Scarlett's heart sank when she caught sight of the baby otter still trembling behind the bucket of fish. "He hasn't even moved! He's probably too scared to know what to do." She leaned sideways, trying to get a better view of the men.

"What's that animal in the water?" said Lily suddenly.

Scarlett pushed a branch aside to look. "It's a black bear! They often catch fish in this part of the river. That must be why they've stopped the boat – the bear's in the way."

The men shouted at the bear to move, waving their fishing rods. The bear stared back grumpily, not moving an inch. The girls slipped from tree to tree until they reached the water's edge.

"Sparky!" whispered Scarlett. "We're over here. Jump off the boat and swim!"

Sparky's whiskers twitched as he saw the girls.

Zina leaned down and gently splashed her hand in the river. Scarlett and Lily joined in.

Sparky's eyes brightened. Then with a flick of his tail, he leapt into the water and swam towards them.

Scarlett's heart skipped. "That's it, Sparky. Swim as fast as you can!"

The men noticed the otter's sudden movement before spotting the girls on the riverbank.

"You again!" snarled the grey-haired man. "You're always following us." He grabbed the wheel of the boat, turning it so sharply that his friend stumbled sideways. The boat tipped a little and the bucket of fish and the rucksack full of stolen things toppled into the river.

The man in the baseball cap groaned. Leaning over the side, he tried to snatch up the bag but it sank below the water. "Give me that fishing rod!"

Both men flicked their fishing rods at the water over and over, but they didn't even manage to catch the fish bucket.

"This is your fault!" yelled the grey-haired man.

"You're the one that made the boat tip!" shouted the other.

The bear shook its head, upset by all the shouting and the waving fishing rods. Rearing up on two legs, it gave a roar so loud that the ground seemed to quiver.

The men jumped. One of them started the engine and the boat sped back upstream. The bear growled even louder but once the boat had gone the animal lumbered out of the river and disappeared into the bushes on the opposite bank.

Sparky swam to the water's edge and leapt out, squeaking happily.

"Sparky, you're safe!" Scarlett stroked his wet fur and he nuzzled her hand.

"Good boy!" said Zina, scratching the baby otter behind his ears. "Don't worry – we'll get you back home."

"And after that we need to go back to the castle and tell the grown-ups all about King Bruno and what he did," added Scarlett.

Lily moved closer to the water's edge. "We might not want to go back just yet."

Scarlett looked up. "Why? I hope those men aren't coming back!"

"No, it isn't them." Lily shaded her eyes. "It's really strange... There's something happening in the river."

A sparkling red light shone below the clear water. It was close to where the boat had been. As the girls watched, the light slipped a little further down the river.

"It looks beautiful!" said Lily.

"What do you think it is?" asked Zina.

Scarlett's heart beat faster. "I'm not sure …
but I think it might be magic!"

Chapter Eleven

The Brightest Jewel

Zina scooped Sparky into her arms and held him tight. The princesses hurried along the bank, following the strange glowing light, but each time they got close it would slip a little further downstream.

"The water's shallow here so maybe we can catch it." Scarlett skidded down the riverbank and leapt into the water.

Lily jumped in with a splash and waded after Scarlett. The round pebbles on the riverbed felt smooth beneath their feet and

the water only came up to their knees. They hurried towards the glowing red light just as it floated away again.

"It's being pushed along by the river," said Lily. "I wish we had a fishing net."

Scarlett noticed a stick drifting by and grabbed it. Then, as soon as she was close enough, she pushed the stick towards the light. Something pulled against the piece of wood and she wobbled, so Lily grabbed her arms to keep her steady. She pulled up the stick and the rucksack lifted out of the water, hooked by one of the straps.

"It's the bag with the stolen things!" gasped Lily. "But why is it glowing?"

Scarlett opened the dripping rucksack, which was filled with jewellery. Queen Freda's diamond bracelet was there and so was Scarlett's emerald tiara. At the bottom of the bag she found her special ruby, which was glowing brighter than fire. "Look at this

– it was my ruby shining!"

"Wow!" breathed Lily. "I guess your jewel-making tools worked after all."

"I guess they did! I made the jewel into a perfect eight-sided shape just like the one in the drawing and that set the magic free." Scarlett gazed at the glowing gem. After a few moments the glow faded, but as soon as she dipped the ruby in the water it shone again.

"The magic comes out when the jewel is under the water!" cried Lily.

Scarlett smiled. "My cousin Ella told me that different jewels have different kinds of magic. I think it's amazing!"

They carried the rucksack and the ruby to the bank to show Zina, who was waiting there with a very tired Sparky.

"You know what this means!" Scarlett's face shone with excitement.

"It means we can give Queen Freda her jewellery back?" suggested Zina.

"Yes! AND now we have all the things we need to be proper Rescue Princesses," said Scarlett, beaming.

The princesses crossed the river where the water was shallow before walking back towards the castle. They let Sparky go beside the pool with the waterfall and watched the other otters bound out of their burrow – their eyes bright and their whiskers twitching.

"Bye, Sparky!" Scarlett gave the baby otter one more stroke. "I'll come back and visit you very soon."

Sparky snuffled at Scarlett's hand. Then he paddled across the water, climbed on to his mother's tummy and stretched out happily. His brothers and sisters all joined paws while lying on their backs in the water.

"I didn't know they slept like that," said Zina.

"It's ever so cute, isn't it?" Scarlett smiled.

"They hold paws to make sure they don't drift away from each other when they're asleep."

When the girls reached the castle, most of the kings and queens were gathered in the parlour, looking worried. Scarlett slipped the ruby into her pocket as they went inside.

Queen Ruth's mouth dropped open when she saw her daughter. "Scarlett, what have you been doing? You're absolutely soaking wet! You really must take better care of your clothes – even when you're just wearing leggings."

Scarlett was too happy to mind being told off. "Sorry! But guess what? We found the stolen jewellery and we know who took it in the first place." She held up the wet rucksack. "We saw King Bruno throw this bag with all the jewels over the castle wall and two men took it away." She told them about the boat they'd seen and how the men had said they were just fishing when they were really waiting for the stolen goods.

Lily chipped in, telling everyone how the men had dropped the bag in the river by mistake. "But we found it and brought it back," she finished proudly. "Because we're Res—"

Scarlett realised what she was about to say and gave her a nudge.

"Oh!" Lily went red as she realised she'd nearly told everyone their secret. "I mean we're res ... resourceful!"

"You certainly are!" King Philip's eyebrows rose. "You've shown quick thinking and determination. I'm very proud of you all."

The royal guests began talking all at once. Queen Freda smiled as Scarlett fished her gold necklace and diamond bracelet from the bag.

"Mr Ellis!" called Queen Ruth. "Tell the guards to find King Bruno right away please."

The butler coughed. "They've just caught him trying to sneak out of the main gate, Your

Highness, and they're bringing him here now. Strangely, it seems he may not be King Bruno at all." He took an envelope from his pocket. "I found this letter when I was cleaning his room this morning. It's a reply to your invitation saying he isn't able to come."

The queen frowned. "Do you mean that man is only *pretending* to be King Bruno?"

"Exactly, Your Majesty!" The butler bowed. "He must have come in the king's place, planning to steal things during his stay."

"I thought I didn't recognise him!" Queen Ruth shook her head. "King Bruno never had a beard like that. Well, that man is going to the police and the guards can look for his friends with the boat too."

"Excuse me!" Lily dropped a curtsy, her fair hair bouncing on her shoulders. "But now that's all sorted out, can we have Scarlett's birthday lunch? I really want to give her my present!"

Chapter Twelve

The Perfect Birthday

Mr Ellis set out a long row of tables in the garden under the trees. Scarlett, Lily and Zina carried out some chairs and set the table with plates, cups and a jug full of pink lemonade.

"Are there any sausage rolls and raspberry jellies and those little butterfly cakes with cream inside?" Scarlett said hopefully.

The butler's face broke into a rare smile. "Of course, Princess Scarlett! I shall fetch all your favourite things. It is your birthday, after all."

Just then Cook brought out Scarlett's

birthday cake – an enormous chocolate cake decorated with icing stars which had nine red candles on top.

Two younger princesses, who'd been playing tag on the grass nearby, came over to gaze at the wonderful cake.

"That looks amazing!" said the taller one. "I'm Taylor and this is Bailey." She pointed to her younger sister.

"Happy birthday!" said Bailey, shyly.

"Thank you!" Scarlett smiled. "Cook, do you think we could all have some of the cake right now?"

Queen Ruth came outside, carrying a vase of roses for the table. "No, of course you can't! We're saving it till the end of lunch." She looked at the table and smiled. "Thank you for helping to get everything ready, girls. Now, hurry along and get changed. You can't attend a royal birthday party in muddy T-shirts and leggings!"

"I wish I could!" sighed Scarlett as they went inside. "I much prefer leggings, and my tiara always digs into my head." She rushed to her bedroom and put the enchanted ruby safely in a drawer. Then she pulled on her best dress – the green one with the velvet ribbon – before adding her emerald tiara.

Lily knocked on the door and came in wearing a long blue dress with a silver tiara on top of her blonde hair.

Scarlett's eyes lit up when she saw the parcel wrapped in pink paper under Lily's arm. "Is that for me?"

Lily nodded and grinned.

Zina came in wearing a pretty white dress and a diamond tiara. "I've got a present for you too, Scarlett." She handed Scarlett a parcel and smiled shyly.

"Thank you!" Scarlett pulled the wrapping paper off Zina's present to reveal a silver box labelled *Make Your Own Rings Set*. Inside was a handful of silver and gold rings.

"It's for making your own rings and decorating them," explained Zina.

"Thank you!" Scarlett beamed. "I love making things."

"And here's my present!" Lily handed Scarlett her parcel.

Scarlett tore open the paper to find a collection of different jewels gathered together in a blue silk scarf. The gems glittered against the cloth like multicoloured stars. "Wow, they're beautiful!"

"Zina told me about the *Make Your Own Rings Set* she was giving you," said Lily. "So I persuaded my mum that we should give you these. You do like them, don't you?"

"I love them!" Scarlett hugged her friends. "Now I can make our magic Rescue Princesses rings. We can use them to call each other if there's an animal in trouble."

"Scarlett, come down!" Queen Ruth called

up the stairs. "We're ready for your birthday lunch."

"That's my mum!" Scarlett jumped up. "We'd better go."

The princesses hurried downstairs, giggling, and headed out into the garden for the special feast.

"This is the best birthday ever!" said Scarlett. "I can't wait for our next Rescue Princesses adventure!"

Look out for another
daring animal adventure!

Chapter One

The Castle of Mistberg Forest

Princess Emily leaned right out of the carriage window, trying to get her first glimpse of the famous castle of Mistberg forest.

She'd waited nine years for her chance to visit and she couldn't wait a second longer. The forest air swept over her, sending her crown slipping sideways and her red curls flapping.

"Emily! Please don't push your head out of the window in that manner. It doesn't look

very graceful," said her mum, straightening her own crown.

Princess Emily took one last look, then reluctantly drew her head back in. "You should have let me drive. I could have gone much faster than this."

Her dad's mouth twitched into a smile.

"The aim is to arrive in royal style," said her mum. "Not to shoot along like a racing car."

Emily resisted saying that racing would be more fun. Her mum and dad were the King and Queen of Middingland and they always knew the correct way to do things.

They had flown across the sea from Middingland that morning in the royal jet. Then they had ridden from the airfield in a carriage, because everyone arrived at the Mistberg Grand Ball by horse and carriage. The Ball took place at King Gudland's castle every spring and was one of the biggest

events of the season.

The scent of pine trees filled the carriage and Emily caught a flash of movement as a deer ran deeper into the forest. The horses pulling the carriage slowed down to a walk as they passed between a pair of gigantic golden gates.

The call of a peacock echoed across the grass. Emily held her breath. They must be inside the grounds of the castle! She stuck her head out of the window again, her heart drumming with excitement.

"Now, when we get inside we have a dress fitting at two o'clock," said the queen. "And you will remember to brush your hair, won't you? It's gone a bit wild in the breeze."

But Emily wasn't thinking about brushing her hair. Above her towered the round turrets of King Gudland's castle, stretching up to the sky.

Usually her little sister would have nudged

her out of the way, but Lottie was staying with their cousins to recover from a bout of chickenpox, so for once, Emily had a perfect view.

The castle was much more magnificent than their palace in Middingland and she had three whole days to explore it.

A short, white-haired man hurried down the flight of steps as the carriage drew to a halt.

"Philip! Maria! How lovely to see you!" he exclaimed.

"Hermann, how are you?" said Emily's mum, stepping gracefully down from the carriage. She turned to her daughter. "Emily, I'd like you to meet King Gudland."

"A pleasure to meet you, Princess," said King Gudland.

Emily made a curtsy. She instantly liked the small man with his twinkly eyes. She hoped all the other kings and queens were

as friendly as he was.

The purpose of the Mistberg Grand Ball was for young princes and princesses, aged nine or older, to present themselves to the twenty royal families from around the world.

Emily had never been before because her parents had been so busy with their royal duties at home in the kingdom of Middingland. But this year was different; Emily was now old enough to take part in the ceremony.

In three days' time she would have to curtsy in front of each and every king and queen, and she was already a little nervous.

"Come this way, Your Majesties," said King Gudland, and he led them through an enormous hallway full of people hurrying around with suitcases.

They climbed up five spiralling staircases watched by the solemn pictures of King Gudland's ancestors. When they reached the

top the king waved his hand towards three wooden doors.

"This is the West Tower, with my very comfiest rooms," he said. "The banquet begins at six o'clock. Don't be late!" And he gave Emily another twinkly smile before stepping back down the staircase.

"That's your room, Emily," said her mum, pointing to the first door. "Meet me in the dressmaking suite in half an hour. It's two staircases down and then turn right. You can't miss it."

Emily nodded, pushed her door open and took her first look at her room. A four-poster bed filled one corner and a soft, velvety sofa sat in the other. But Emily was drawn to the window, and when she got closer she realised that she was very near the top of the tower.

Everything on the ground looked tiny. She could see the stables for King Gudland's horses and a set of obstacles that looked like a huge adventure playground.

As she stared down, another carriage drew up in front of the castle and a girl dressed in green climbed out.

Emily watched her eagerly. She was looking forward to meeting some more princesses of her own age. Life at home in her palace in Middingland was great, but there was only her little sister to play with.

Suddenly Emily looked at her watch. Half an hour had flown by while she was daydreaming at the window. She was supposed to be in the dressmaking suite with her mum right now!